THE GNOME FROM NOME

Written By:
STEPHEN COSGROVE

Illustrated By:
ROBIN JAMES

GROLIER ENTERPRISES INC.
Danbury, Connecticut

A Serendipity Book

Dedicated to the people of Alaska who taught me that love truly is warm.

S. Cosgrove

The coldest place in all the world is far north of everywhere, and is simply called the North Pole. It is so cold, nothing much lives there except for one small creature . . . a lonely gnome.

Now let me tell you, that gnome was cold. In fact he was so cold living there at the North Pole that his ears were a frosty pink, and his nose was a bright, bright blue. He would scream, shout and stomp just trying to get warm.

For you see, the gnome was cold from the inside out. "If I shout," he shouted, "the cold will get out and not stay in!" Sure enough, every time he would shout or scream, a puff of white cold would come out. But still the gnome was not warm from the inside out.

One day that gnome could stand it no longer and decided to head south, where it just had to be warmer.

He got together all his belongings: his icicle toothbrush, his favorite purple pajamas with the furry feet, and his magic paint set given to him by the Master of the Northern Lights. He packed them in his knapsack and set off for the south.

He walked, shouted, skittered and skated for days until he came to what is today called Alaska. Much to his dismay, he was just as cold there as he had been at the North Pole. "Darn!" he screamed. "I'm too tired to go on and I'm still freezing."

Then the gnome spotted all the branches and sticks lying around. "Maybe," he thought loudly, "if I light a fire I can get warm." So he set about collecting wood and building the biggest bonfire you have ever seen.

The gnome stood away from the fire and waited to get warm, but nothing happened. So he stood a little closer, and still nothing happened. Finally he did what you are never supposed to do, and stood so close to the fire that his beard began to smolder.

"Oh no!" he shouted, and jumped head-first into a snowbank to put out his smoldering beard.

That poor gnome felt so dejected he just sat on a frosty log and began to cry large frozen tears.

"Oh dear!" he shouted, "There must be no way in the world for me to get warm from the inside out."

As he sat there crying, a sea otter happened by, shaking and shivering and wearing a heavy plaid scarf. "Why are you crying?" shivered the otter. "Because I am so cold!" shouted the gnome. "Then why are you shouting?" chattered the otter. "Because," yelled the gnome, "when I shout it gets part of the cold from the inside out!"

The otter thought for a moment, then tilted his head back and shouted just as loud as he could. Sure enough, out came a puff of cold. Then, in cold silence, the two of them just sat there on the log, shivering, shaking and shouting, and trying to figure out how to get warm from the inside out.

"You know," yelled the otter, "in my travels I've noticed that humans are never cold from the inside out. Maybe if we were around them we could learn their secret."

"We've got to get them to come to us," chattered the gnome. "I'm so cold, I don't think I could walk another step."

They sat and thought and thought, and finally the gnome came up with a plan. "All humans like gold!" he shouted. "I'll use the magic paint given to me by the Master of the Northern Lights and turn everything into gold! Then when the humans come, we'll ask them for their secret in exchange for the gold!"

The gnome rummaged around in his knap-sack until he found his magic can of golden paint. Then he and the otter began painting everything gold. When they were all done, they stood back and looked at what they had painted.

"With all the gold around, those humans should tell us their secret," chattered the gnome. So he and the otter set out to tell the humans.

The two of them climbed the highest mountain around. While the otter looked on, the gnome shouted at the top of his voice, "Gold, gold! We've discovered gold!"

I don't know if you've ever heard a gnome shout, but if you have you'll know what I mean when I say his voice carried for miles and miles. There wasn't a human within a thousand miles who didn't know that there was gold in Alaska.

The gnome and the otter ran down to the edge of their valley to wait for the secret that would make them warm from the inside out.

Humans were already beginning to arrive by the hundreds, but they just ignored the gnome and the otter.

"Won't somebody please tell us the secret of how to be warm from the inside out?" shivered and shouted the frozen gnome.

But no one would stop. In fact they pushed that poor gnome and the frozen otter right into a snowbank. Those humans were picking up all of that gold and didn't even notice the gnome and the otter.

Just about then a prospector happened by and he saw the two sitting in the snow. "Who are you?" asked the prospector. "And why are you not picking up any gold?"

"I'm the gnome, and this is the otter," shivered the gnome. "We don't need gold. We made it so you would come here and tell us the secret of being warm from the inside out, but everyone has just ignored us."

The prospector thought for a moment and then said, "Wait here. I'll be right back." Then he hurried off to talk with the other prospectors.

He hustled and bustled about until he had gathered all of the humans together. "Fellow prospectors," he began from the top of a stump. "We're getting rich picking up all of this gold. The only reason the gold is here is because of those two creatures sitting in yonder snowbank. Now we simply must come up with an answer to their problem!"

All the humans murmured and mumbled, fretted and fumed until they finally figured out what to do.

With cheers and shouts they all marched back to the gnome and the otter.

"We have unanimously decided," said the prospector, "to tell you the secret of keeping warm from the inside out."

The gnome and the otter could not believe their good fortune and listened very carefully. "The reason that humans are warm from the inside out is because of love and friendship. That is the secret!"

"But how do we get love and friendship?" asked the otter through chattering teeth. The prospector thought for a moment and then continued. "Friendship means the state of being friends with someone. Since you are in Alaska, you and the gnome already are in that state!"

The gnome and the otter looked at one another and realized that the prospector was right. They began to warm from the inside out.

Then the gnome asked, "But what about love? Where do we find that?"

"You have already shown love by bringing us this gift of gold," said the prospector. "We are your friends, and as a token of our appreciation and love we hereby name this town in your honor." With that, two miners brought out a large sign which read: "Nome, Alaska, Population 2."

The gnome and the otter were so elated that they didn't even mind that the miners had misspelled gnome.

"It's working!" laughed the gnome. "I'm beginning to feel all warm and toasty inside." "Me too!" said the otter. "To think that all this time the secret has been right under our noses...in our hearts!"

So the gnome from Nome and his new found friend the sea otter returned to the North Pole. They live there to this very day, wrapped up warmly in love and friendship, sipping tea . . . and talking very softly.

So when you're cold
From the inside out
And don't know what to do,
Remember love and friendship,
And warmth will come to you.